Other Kipper Books

Kipper
Kipper and Roly
Kipper's A to Z: An Alphabet Adventure
Kipper's Birthday
Kipper's Christmas Eve
Kipper's Snowy Day
Kipper's Toybox
Where, Oh Where, Is Kipper's Bear?
Kipper's Book of Colors
Kipper's Book of Numbers

Kipper's Book of Opposites
Kipper's Book of Weather
Kipper Has a Party (Sticker Story)
Kipper in the Snow (Sticker Story)
Kipper and the Egg (Touch and Feel)
Kipper's Sticky Paws (Touch and Feel)
Kipper's Lost Ball (Lift the Flap)
Kipper's Rainy Day (Lift the Flap)
Kipper's Sunny Day (Lift the Flap)
Kipper's Tree House (Lift the Flap)

Little Kippers

Arnold
Butterfly
Hissss!
Honk!
Meow!
Picnic

Rocket
Sandcastle
Skates
Splosh!
Swing!
Thing!

www.harcourt.com

First published in Great Britain in 2002 by Hodder Children's Books, a division of Hodder Headline Limited
First Red Wagon Books edition 2002

Red Wagon Books is a trademark of Harcourt, Inc., registered in the
United States of America and/or other jurisdictions.

Library of Congress Cataloging-in-Publication Data
Inkpen, Mick.
Kipper's monster/Mick Inkpen.
p. cm.
Summary: While camping out in the woods, Kipper and Tiger
encounter a horrendous "monster" which is not what it seems.
[1. Dogs—Fiction. 2. Monsters—Fiction. 3. Camping—Fiction.] I. Title.
PZ7.I564Kjjm 2002
[E]—dc21 2001003354
ISBN 0-15-216614-9

A C E G H F D B

Printed in Hong Kong

Kipper's Monster

Mick Inkpen

Red Wagon Books
Harcourt, Inc.
San Diego   New York   London

Tiger had a brand-new flashlight.
"It's the most powerful flashlight
there is!" he said to Kipper.
He shone it at Big Owl.
He shone it at Hippo.
He shone it in Kipper's face.
"You should see it when it's
dark!" he said. "It's REALLY good
when it's dark!"

Tiger sat in Kipper's basket
and pulled the blanket over
his head.

"Come on! We can make it dark
under here!" he said.

Under the blanket was one of
Kipper's storybooks.

"That's another thing!" said Tiger.
"You can read under the covers
with a flashlight like this!"

Kipper began to read.
"Deep in the middle of the
dark, dark wood, there lived a horrible,
horrendous, terrible, tremendous..."

"That's it!" shouted Tiger,
jumping up. "We'll camp in the woods
tonight! It'll be really, REALLY dark in
the woods."

"Shall I bring my
book?" said Kipper.

So they took the book and some cookies, and they put up their tent in the middle of the woods at the bottom of Big Hill.

But as it got dark, Tiger began to think that perhaps this wasn't such a good idea after all.

"Come inside and have a cookie," said Kipper. "Do you want Rabbit or Big Owl?"

But Tiger didn't reply. He was looking nervously out of the door.

"Do you think there are any bears in these woods?" he whispered.

"No, I don't think so," said Kipper. He began to read.

"Deep in the middle of the dark, dark wood, there lived a horrible..."

But Tiger wasn't ready. He asked Kipper to sit next to the door, instead of him. And when Kipper tried again to read, Tiger got up and zipped the door shut altogether.

But the third time Kipper tried
to read, from somewhere outside
the tent there came the most terrible,
tremendous, horrible, horrendous

Screech!

"What was that?" said Kipper. Tiger said nothing.

"Let's go and look!" whispered Kipper. So they crept out of the tent and into the woods, shining Tiger's flashlight ahead of them.

"I think it came from somewhere near here," said Kipper. The flashlight lit up the enormous gray trunk of an old tree.

There in the middle was a dark, dark hole.

Suddenly a huge pair of
yellow eyes blinked open, and
from the hole came the most terrible

Screech!

They shrieked and ran, bumping
into each other and sending the
flashlight flying. They scrambled into
the tent and lay there panting hard,
listening. . . .

"I think it was just an owl," whispered Kipper. "Yes, it was just a silly old owl."

But behind him, the shadow of something was growing on the wall of the tent.

Something with horns.

"It's a horrible, horrendous monster!" squealed Tiger.

The shape on the tent grew and grew till it was looming above them. Then it slowly changed into a shape that Kipper had seen before.

Kipper crept back out of the tent and walked toward the flashlight. There, caught in the beam, was a little snail.

Kipper picked up the flashlight and let the snail crawl onto his paw.

He looked at the snail closely. Its horns curled in and out as he touched them.

"I've found the horrible, horrendous monster! Look, Tiger!"

Tiger peeped out from underneath the blanket.

He saw the snail.

He saw its shadow.

He felt silly.

"Shall I read the story now?"
said Kipper.

But Kipper never did get to read his story, because they went home to Tiger's house, where they put up the tent in Tiger's bedroom...

... and Tiger got to read it instead.